READ ALL OF THESE
NATE THE GREAT
DETECTIVE STORIES
BY MARJORIE WEINMAN SHARMAT
WITH ILLUSTRATIONS BY MARC SIMONT:

NATE THE GREAT

NATE THE GREAT GOES UNDERCOVER

NATE THE GREAT AND THE LOST LIST

NATE THE GREAT AND THE PHONY CLUE

NATE THE GREAT AND THE STICKY CASE

NATE THE GREAT AND THE MISSING KEY

NATE THE GREAT AND THE SNOWY TRAIL

NATE THE GREAT AND THE FISHY PRIZE

NATE THE GREAT STALKS STUPIDWEED

NATE THE GREAT AND THE BORING BEACH BAG

NATE THE GREAT GOES DOWN IN THE DUMPS

NATE THE GREAT AND THE HALLOWEEN HUNT

NATE THE GREAT AND THE MUSICAL NOTE
(by Marjorie Weinman Sharmat and Craig Sharmat)

NATE THE GREAT AND THE STOLEN BASE

NATE THE GREAT AND THE PILLOWCASE
(by Marjorie Weinman Sharmat and Rosalind Weinman)

NATE THE GREAT AND THE MUSHY VALENTINE

Nate the Great and The Mushy Valentine

by
Marjorie Weinman Sharmat
illustrations by Marc Simont

Delacorte  Press

Published by Delacorte Press
Bantam Doubleday Dell Publishing Group, Inc.
1540 Broadway
New York, New York 10036

Library of Congress Cataloging in Publication Data
Sharmat, Marjorie Weinman.
    Nate the Great and the mushy valentine / by Marjorie Sharmat;
illustrated by Marc Simont.
    p.   cm.
    Summary: Nate the Great investigates two cases that may be connected, involving a missing valentine and a valentine that came from nowhere.
    ISBN 0-385-31166-4
    [1. Valentine's Day—Fiction.   2. Mystery and detective stories.]
I. Simont, Marc, ill   II. Title.
PZ7.S5299Naui   1994
[E]—dc20   93-15488   CIP   AC

Manufactured in the United States of America
February 1994
10 9 8 7 6 5 4 3 2 1
WOR

For my two Nates:

For you, my grandson,
Nathan Sharmat,
born December 12, 1992

And in memory of your
great-grandfather,
Nathan Weinman,
born one hundred years earlier
on July 12, 1892

Always remember, Nate is great!

y name is Nate the Great.
I am a detective.
I have a dog, Sludge.
He is a detective too.
He helps me with my cases.
But one day I had to help
Sludge with his case.

It was Valentine's Day.
Sludge was napping
in his doghouse.
I tiptoed up to it.
I saw a big red paper heart
taped to the outside of the house.
Something was printed on the heart.
I LOVE YOU SLUDGE
MORE THAN FUDGE
Someone had given Sludge
a valentine!
I was glad that no one had given me
a valentine.
I, Nate the Great, do not like
mushy words.
Or slushy words.
I, Nate the Great, do not want to be
anyone's valentine.

Sludge came out of his doghouse.
I showed him his valentine.
It was signed with initials.
ABH.
"Who is ABH?" I asked Sludge.
Sludge sniffed the valentine.
And sniffed it.
He did not know who it was from either.
He looked at me.

"You want me to help you
find out who sent you
this valentine?" I asked.
"This is not my kind of case."
But Sludge is my kind of dog.
I wrote a note to my mother.

Dear Mother,
I am on a Valentine case.
Somebody loves Sludge
more than fudge.
When I find out who
I will be back.
Love,
Nate the Great

Sludge and I looked for
footprints around his doghouse.
Sludge carried his valentine
in his mouth
while he looked.
He liked it.
We did not see any footprints.
I was thinking,
What clues do I have?

The printing on the valentine
was made with stencils.
Anybody could have done it.
And anybody could have
stuck the valentine
on the doghouse.
Who do Sludge and I know?
We know Rosamond, Oliver, Claude,
Annie, Annie's little brother Harry,
Esmeralda, Pip, and Finley.
None of them have the initials ABH.
I saw Annie and her dog, Fang,
coming toward us.
Fang will never be anybody's
valentine.
"I have a case for you," Annie said.
"I can't find a valentine that I made.
Please look for it."

"I already have a valentine case,"
I said. "Somebody gave Sludge
a valentine, but we don't know who.
I, Nate the Great,
take only one case at a time."
"I must find my valentine,"
Annie said. *"Please."*
I wrote another note to my mother.

Dear Mother
Two Valentine cases.
I will be back.
Love,
Nate the Great

"Tell me about your missing valentine," I said to Annie.

"This morning Rosamond and I each made a valentine at my house," Annie said. "Rosamond called them valentwins."

"Valentwins?"

"Yes, because her valentine and my valentine looked exactly alike. We each cut out a big red paper heart. We each printed I LOVE YOU on our hearts."

"Then what happened?" I asked.

"Rosamond went home with her valentine," Annie said. "I began to sign my name on mine. I was going to give it to my little brother Harry.

But Fang came into my room.
He looked hungry."
I, Nate the Great,
knew that look very well.
"Fang and I went to the kitchen,"
Annie said. "I gave him some kibbles.
When I got back to my room,
my valentine was gone."

"Did Rosamond tell you who she was making her valentine for?" I asked.

"No," Annie said. "What does that have to do with my case?"

"Nothing," I said. "But I am on two cases at the same time. Remember?" I pointed to Sludge. "Please look at the valentine Sludge is carrying. Does that look like the ones that you and Rosamond made?"

"Yes," Annie said. "Except that there's more printed on this one. And this one also has initials. Rosamond's valentine and my valentine just said I LOVE YOU."

"But then you started to sign yours," I said.

"Yes, but I didn't get very far,"
Annie said.

"*You* may not have gotten very far,"
I said, "but Rosamond could have
printed much more on *her* valentine
when she got home. I, Nate the Great,

say that Rosamond made her
valentine for Sludge."
"Why would she do that?"
Annie asked.
"Only Rosamond knows," I said.
"Last year she made a valentine
for the man in the moon."
"So you have solved your case,"
Annie said.
"Not quite," I said.
"Sludge's valentine
was signed with the initials ABH.

Those are not Rosamond's initials.
Why would she print them on her
valentine? Before I solve a case, all the
pieces have to fit."
"Do you have any clues in *my* case?"
Annie asked.
"I don't know. Show me where your
valentine was the last time you saw it."
We all walked to Annie's house.

We went to her room.
She pointed to her desk.
"The valentine was right here,"
she said.
I looked at Annie's desk.
There were pencils
and stencils and paste
and red paper on it.
No valentine.
Sludge was sniffing the desk.
"There are no clues
on this desk,"
I said to him.

But Sludge kept sniffing.
I peered over and under,
in back of, in front of,
and inside of things.
I could not find Annie's valentine.

"Your valentine is not in this room,"
I said. "Tell me, was anybody
in your house besides you and Fang
when your valentine disappeared?"
"Yes," Annie said. "Harry was
in his room."
"Hmm. He could have gone to your
room while you were in the kitchen."
"I suppose," Annie said. "But he
wouldn't have taken the valentine.
He knew I was going to give it to him
right after I finished signing
my name to it."
"Perhaps he was in a hurry to
have it," I said.
"No," Annie said. "Harry doesn't like
valentines."

22

"Then why did you make one for him?"
I asked.

Annie smiled. "I like to give
valentines."

"So you like to give but Harry doesn't
like to get," I said. "That could be
important. Then again, it might not
be important. I must talk to Harry.
Where is he?"

Annie shrugged. "He disappeared
when the valentine disappeared."
"Aha!" I said. "That could be
a big clue. Where does Harry
like to go?"
"He likes to go to Rosamond's house
to play with her Hexes," Annie said.
"Her Hexes?"
"You know, Rosamond's cats.
She has a Super Hex, a Big Hex,
a Plain Hex, and a Little Hex."
"Yes," I said. "Rosamond has a Hex
for all occasions."

Suddenly I, Nate the Great, thought
of something.
"I have just solved the case," I said.
"Oh, great," Annie said. "Where is
my valentine?"
"No, not your case. Sludge's case.
I have not been thinking strange enough.
If I had, I would have known that
the pieces fit. I must speak to
Rosamond."
"And look for Harry," Annie said.
I, Nate the Great, do not like
to go to Rosamond's house.
But now I had two reasons to go there.
Annie, Sludge, Fang, and I rushed
to Rosamond's house.

Rosamond was sitting on her floor,
making a strange, squishy brown
valentine. Her four cats were crawling
all over her.
"I am on two cases," I said. "I need
Harry for one and you for the other."
"Harry was here playing with my

cats," Rosamond said. "But he left.
I don't know where he went.
But I'm here. Why do you need me?"
I took Sludge's valentine
from his mouth.

27

I handed it to Rosamond.

"I, Nate the Great, say that you made this valentine for Sludge and signed it ABH. Those are the initials for *A Big Hex*. This valentine was from Big Hex to Sludge, right?"

"Wrong," Rosamond said. "This valentine looks like the one I made, except for the Sludge part and the initials."

"You didn't add words or initials to yours?" I asked.

"I added words," Rosamond said. "But these are not the words. Besides, I would never do a strange thing

like make a valentine
for a cat to give to a dog."
Rosamond would do even stranger
things, but I did not want to
go into that.
"I made my valentine for a
person," Rosamond said, "but
it's a secret who. Right now
I am making a valentine out of liver
for my cats. They haven't
been eating their liver lately.

It's too good to throw away,
so I am changing it into
something different.
Want to watch my cats
eat their valentine?"
It was time to leave.
I said to Annie, "Go to your house
and wait there,
in case Harry comes back."
Sludge and I went home.
"I have to eat pancakes,"
I said to Sludge. "I have to think.
I have to think twice as hard
as I would if I had only
one case to solve."
I made some pancakes.
I gave Sludge a bone.
I thought about Sludge's case.

Sludge is a great dog.
Everybody loves him.
Anybody could have given him
the valentine.
That was no help to me.

I thought about Annie's case.
The only person who
could have taken the valentine
meant for Harry
was Harry.
But Annie said that Harry
doesn't like valentines.
I made more pancakes.
What had I learned at
Rosamond's house?
I learned what she did with liver
that her cats didn't want.

If that was a clue, it was a strange one.
What had I learned at Annie's house?
Sludge had kept sniffing
at Annie's desk.
Where her valentine had been.
Was that a clue?
Perhaps.
But what case was it a clue for?
Sludge's case?

Or Annie's case?

Or *both*?

Did it matter?

Perhaps I could use a clue from
one case to help solve another case!

I picked up Sludge's valentine
where he had dropped it
while he chewed his bone.

There *had* to be a reason
why Sludge's valentine looked
like Annie's and Rosamond's.

But Rosamond said she had made hers
for a secret person.

And Annie said she had made hers
for her brother Harry.

I stared at the initials ABH.

I now knew they didn't mean
A Big Hex.

But they had to be *somebody's* initials.
Who would sign ABH?
Suddenly I, Nate the Great, had a lot
of pieces that fit.
"We must go back to Annie's house,"
I said.
Sludge dropped his bone and
picked up his valentine.
We went to Annie's house.

Sludge sniffed Annie's desk again.
"I have solved your case,"
I said to Annie. "See how
Sludge is sniffing your desk.
That's because *his* valentine
was once on your desk.
His valentine was *your*
valentine."

"What?" Annie said.
"How much of your name did you
print on your valentine before
you had to stop?" I asked.
"Just A," Annie said. "I was going
to finish with NNIE."

"I, Nate the Great, say that your
brother Harry saw the valentine
you made for him. He didn't want
it. So he added the words
SLUDGE MORE THAN FUDGE.
Then he added B and H to the A
you had signed. ABH stands for
Annie's Brother Harry. Then he
took the valentine to Sludge's
doghouse and stuck it there."

"But why didn't he just throw away
the valentine instead of doing all
of that?" Annie asked.

"For the same reason Rosamond
could not throw away the liver,"
I said. "Remember when she told us
it was too good to throw away,
so she changed it into something
different? Harry did not want to
throw away something good either:

the valentine you made for him.
So he changed it into something
different . . . a valentine for Sludge."
"But why Sludge?" Annie asked.
"Look how much Sludge likes it,"
I said. "Harry had a very good idea."
"I will never make another valentine
for Harry," Annie said.
"Harry will be glad to hear that,"
I said. I turned to go.
I had solved Annie's case.
I had solved Sludge's case.
They were the same case.
Sludge and I walked home.
I saw something
stuck to my front door.

It was a big red paper heart.
I had gotten a valentine after all!
I knew who it was from.
I knew what I did not want
to know.
I was Rosamond's secret person.
I walked up to the door.
I, Nate the Great,
was about to read that
Rosamond loves me.
I was not ready for that.
I would never be ready for that.
But I had to face it.
I read I LOVE YOU NATE
BECAUSE YOU'RE GREAT.
I had to take this valentine
off my door!

But if I touched it,
it would be mine.
Perhaps the valentine would fall off
by itself.
Or blow away.
Rot.
Die.

I, Nate the Great, could wait.
I stepped backward.
I knew another house
where I could wait.
Sludge was very glad to have me.

PROSPECT FREE LIBRARY
915 Trenton Falls Road
Prospect, New York 13435

MEMBER

MID-YORK LIBRARY SYSTEM
Utica, N.Y. 13502